The
TINY ANGEL

Story and Pictures

by

Elizabeth Koda-Callan

WORKMAN PUBLISHING, NEW YORK

The design/logo, including the words "Elizabeth Koda-Callan's Magic Charm Books," is a registered trademark of Elizabeth Koda-Callan.

"Magic Charm Books" and "Elizabeth Koda-Callan's Magic Charm Books" are trademarks of Elizabeth Koda-Callan.

Library of Congress Cataloging-in-Publication Data

Koda-Callan, Elizabeth.
The tiny angel : story and pictures
by Elizabeth Koda-Callan.

p.   cm.

Summary: The inspiration of a shimmering angel charm helps the youngest singer in a Christmas pageant discover strength in herself. Includes a golden angel charm on a chain, tucked into the cover of the book.

ISBN 1-56305-120-6

1. Toy and movable books—Specimens. [1. Self-confidence—Fiction.
2. Singing—Fiction. 3. Christmas—Fiction. 4. Angels—Fiction.
5. Toy and movable books.] I. Title.
PZ.K8175Ti 1991   91-50386
[E]—dc20   CIP
                                                                        AC

Workman books are available at special discounts when purchased in bulk for premiums and sales promotions as well as for fund-raising or educational use. Special editions or book excerpts can also be created to specification. For details, contact the Special Sales Director at the address below.

Workman Publishing Company
708 Broadway
New York, New York 10003-9555

Printed in China

First Printing October 1991

For Ava, Eloise, and Hayley

And always for Jennifer

Once there was a little girl who longed to be an angel in her school's Christmas pageant. She wanted to be the angel who delivered the message of Christmas.

The little girl was excited when the teacher announced the tryouts for the pageant. She knew just the part she wanted.

The auditions took place the follow-
ing week. The little girl was so nervous
that she stammered when she read her
lines, and her voice became small and
quiet.

When the auditions were over, the little
girl was assigned to be an angel in the
chorus.

Later that day, her mother asked the little girl why she looked so sad. "I don't want to be in the Christmas pageant," she said.

Her mother was surprised. "Why not?" she asked.

"I didn't get the part I wanted. Instead, I'm the littlest angel in the chorus. My voice gets lost among the other voices," the little girl said. "I wanted a speaking part, but I stammer when I read my lines."

"In a chorus every voice is important, no matter how small," her mother said. "One voice works with another. That's what creates harmony and makes the music so beautiful. Besides, everyone will be counting on you."

The little girl thought about what her mother had said. She wasn't happy, but she agreed to be in the chorus.

Before the little girl's first rehearsal, her mother came up with a surprise. "Here's something that might help you see your part differently," her mother said, handing the little girl a small white box with a golden ribbon. The little girl untied the ribbon and opened the box. There, resting on cotton as soft as a cloud, was a tiny angel on a gold chain.

"You may be the littlest angel, but you can also be the brightest," her mother said. "This necklace will help you be the best angel for the part."

The little girl admired the necklace. "It would be nice to shine as brightly as this tiny angel," she thought.

FA, LA, LA, LA, LA, LA, LA, LA, LA, . . .

Each week the little girl went to chorus practice. At every practice session she wore her angel necklace. The sessions were

tiring. There were many notes to sing, and the chorus had to practice them over and over again.

At times her voice cracked.

At times she was off-key. Days passed,
and the little girl struggled on.

The little girl soon learned the words and melodies to the songs. She even sang on her way home from school. Still, her voice was unsteady.

The one day she began to listen more closely to the voices around her. Some of them were strong voices. As if somehow encouraged by them, she found herself joining them and singing more forcefully. Her own voice became stronger. She became more confident. And she began to enjoy singing in the chorus.

The day of the performance arrived. The little girl was excited and just a little bit nervous. She put on a gown of satin and her mother helped her with golden angel wings and a golden halo. Around her neck, she wore her angel necklace.

After she finished dressing, the little girl and her parents drove to school.

The air buzzed with excitement as the children, all dressed in their costumes, gathered backstage. The little girl began to feel even more nervous. She wondered if her voice would be strong enough.

At that moment something unexpected happened. The teacher announced that a child who had a speaking part was sick. "Is there anyone else who knows the lines to this part?" the teacher asked.

The little girl stepped forward. "I do," she said, and she recited the lines. Her voice was clear and steady. She didn't stammer this time.

The teacher looked pleased. "Your voice is much stronger since you've been singing in the chorus. I want you to say the final lines in today's performance."

While waiting to join the other children onstage, the little girl began to think of everything that had changed since the beginning of rehearsals. She had discovered that she enjoyed singing in the chorus. And now she had a speaking part, too.

The little girl remembered what her mother had said. She looked down at her tiny angel necklace. "This little angel has helped me see that even small parts can be important," she thought. "Today I want to shine as brightly as my tiny angel."

Soon it was time for the little girl to join the chorus of angels onstage. When they were in their places, they began to sing. Their voices filled the auditorium as they sang Christmas carols in beautiful harmony.

After the last song, the little girl
stepped forward. A spotlight was on her.
She looked tiny and delicate surrounded

by the vastness of the stage. But in a strong
voice the little girl spoke:

"Peace on earth.
Good will toward all mankind."

It was a special moment for her. She realized that even the littlest angel can shine brightly indeed.

About the Author

Elizabeth Koda-Callan is a graphic designer, illustrator, and children's book author who lives in New York City. Her own holiday season activities include attending Christmas concerts and viewing the Metropolitan Museum's magnificent tree.

She is the creator of the well-loved children's books, THE MAGIC LOCKET, THE SILVER SLIPPERS, and THE GOOD LUCK PONY.